For My Son
ARDEN
Merry Christmas,
Little Critter

LITTLE CRITTER'S®
CHRISTMAS BOOK

BY
MERCER MAYER

A GOLDEN BOOK • NEW YORK

Golden Books Publishing Company, Inc., New York, New York 10106

🌷 A GOLDEN BOOK • NEW YORK

Golden Books Publishing Company, Inc., New York, New York 10106

TABLE OF CONTENTS

Christmas is coming soon. Every year I get ready real early. The first thing I do is write my letter to Santa Claus. Sometimes I write him more than one. Of course, Santa always comes to the store in town, and that way I can go and read him the list of toys I want. Last year I only got to read half of my list, because my mom said it was too long.

Sometimes I almost wait too long to mail my letter to Santa, but I always get it in just in time.

WINTER FUN

Waiting for Christmas to come is hard, but there are a lot of things to do while I wait.

I go skating on the pond.
Mom thinks I need help,
but I don't...

except sometimes.

I go sledding down the hill.

I go fast.

I go faster.

And even faster.

Sometimes I go too fast.

11

I make a snow critter with Mom, Dad, and my little sister.

I throw a snowball at my dad.

12

My dad throws a snowball at me.

My little sister throws a snowball at me.

I throw a snowball at my little sister.
My little sister cries.
Dad says, "It's time to go inside."

Mom makes hot chocolate for everyone. That makes everyone happy, even my little sister.

Mom takes a fresh cake out of the oven. It smells so good, but we can't have any. It's for Christmas.

Mom makes a lot of Christmas desserts.
She is making a lot of cookies.

This time we are lucky...

15

we get to eat the broken cookies and lick the bowls and spoons.

As Christmas gets closer we drive to town to go Christmas shopping.

All the stores are full of presents. If Santa bought his presents at the stores in town, he wouldn't have to spend so much time making them.

My little sister and I like to look in all of the windows, but Dad says it's too cold. When I am looking at new toys, I never get too cold.

TOY TESTING

Inside the store there are so many things I never thought of putting on my list to Santa.

JR. HOCKEY KIT

Manager

This is fun because I can try out all of the different toys.

I wish the store manager wouldn't follow me around, though. Hasn't he ever seen anyone play football?

Oops!

It's hard work trying out new toys.

Some things are not made very well. I certainly wouldn't want that for Christmas.

19

MEETING SANTA

Santa is in the store, and there is a long line to see him. I don't want to wait, but I do because I have more toys to add to my list.

Finally it's my turn to see Santa. Boy, am I glad that I waited. Some little kids cry because they are scared. I guess they don't really want new toys for Christmas. My little sister can't make up her mind about what she wants. That sure is silly.

I find a great present for Mom and Dad. Dad pays for it because all I have is a quarter.

On our way back to the car we stop and look at a manger scene. It makes me feel all warm and snuggly inside.

The closer it gets to Christmas, the harder it is to sleep. I try real hard, but I keep thinking I see Santa and his reindeer.

On the last day of school we have a play.
But first we make Christmas decorations,

paint Christmas pictures,

and make our own Christmas cards.

THE CHRISTMAS PLAY

I am a shepherd in the school play, but I'm not scared...at least not very much.

I have to say, "Behold yon star."
Mom helped me practice so I would remember what to say. I did real good. Mom said so.

THE CHRISTMAS TREE

Finally it's time to cut our Christmas tree. We all get dressed real warm and go out into the woods. Dad always picks the best tree.

We tie it up with ropes and drag it back home through the snow. Mom cuts holly to make a wreath, and my little sister just plays. But what do you expect.

Dad puts the tree in the stand. I help. Mom and my little sister tell us that the tree is crooked.

Dad brings all of the ornaments down from the attic.

We decorate the tree. Dad puts the last decoration on. It's a star, and it goes on the very top. "Don't fall on the tree, Dad!"

Dad doesn't think that is very funny...last year he fell on the tree.

HOW TO WRAP A PRESENT

I know how to wrap a present. Watch me.

1. Cut your wrapping paper just the right size.

2. Wrap the paper around the present and pull off a small piece of tape.

3. Tape the wrapping paper to the present.

4. Then tape the wrapping paper together.

5. Pull off another small piece of tape.

6. Tape down the wrapping paper at both ends so that the present is covered real good.

7. If that doesn't work, call your mom.

DECORATING

We decorate our home for Christmas.
Dad hangs mistletoe.
My little sister draws a picture.
I help Mom decorate the windows.

Mom makes a Christmas wreath for our front door.
I make one for the back door.

CHRISTMAS EVE

Christmas Eve is here. Grandma and Grandpa come to visit.
They bring lots of presents. We have a big dinner and then we
sing Christmas carols.

33

We say good night to Grandma and Grandpa. Tomorrow we will have Christmas dinner at their house. I bet there will be more presents.

Dad says it's time to go to bed, otherwise Santa won't come.

We put out some cookies and milk for Santa, because he most likely gets hungry and thirsty carrying all those presents around.

I check everything once more. Then it's time for bed.

CHRISTMAS SONG

Mom and Dad made up a special Christmas song just for me and my little sister. This is how it goes.

Merry Christmas, Little Critters

Mer - ry Christ - mas, Lit - tle Crit - ters, may all your dreams come true. San - ta

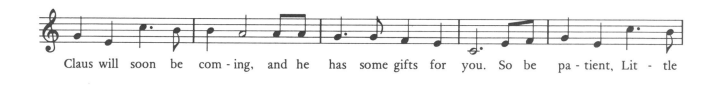

Claus will soon be com - ing, and he has some gifts for you. So be pa - tient, Lit - tle

Crit - ters, and close your sleep - y eyes. Can't you hear the rein - deer a -

cross the star - ry skies? ___ I know you've helped your mom - my, ev - ery

36

time you could you would, and to ev - ery - bod - y you've been kind___ just

like you know you should. Then___ sleep now, Lit - tle Crit - ters, this si - lent Christ - mas

Eve, for___ San - ta's near the Christ - mas tree with the pre - sents that he'll leave.

Soon the morn - ing sun will rise___ to greet the Christ - mas Day, then your

mom and dad's___ lov - ing eyes___ will watch you and they'll say___

"Merry Christmas, Little Critters."

37

THE CHRISTMAS DREAM

It's always so hard to go to sleep on Christmas Eve,

but finally I do.
I have a dream.

It is the night before Christmas and all through the house,

not a Critter is stirring, not even a mouse.

The stockings are hung up.
Each one is red.

And my mom and my dad
have just gone to bed.

39

Then I hear something
that scares me plain silly.

I have to go see, though
the night is so chilly.

I peek round the corner, and to my surprise,
I can barely believe what I see with my eyes.

It is Santa.
He turns and begins to say...

But then I awake.
It's Christmas Day!

41

It's Christmas morning. My little sister and I race each other downstairs. I let her win because she's little. Sure enough, all around the tree are the gifts Santa Claus brought us.

42

One of my new toys doesn't seem to work right, but Dad shows me how to do it. I got everything I wanted, almost. But then Mom says not to be greedy and be happy with what I got.

I never said I wasn't happy, did I?

I wonder if Santa got some of his gifts from the store where I saw him.

Christmas Day is my favorite time. But
it's so tiring playing with all those new toys
that I have to take a rest.

44